The Legend of
Lāʻieikawai

The Legend of
Lā'ieikawai

Retold and illustrated by

Dietrich Varez

A Latitude 20 Book

University of Hawai'i Press
Honolulu

© 2004 University of Hawai'i Press

Printed in the United States of America

09 08 07 06 05 04   6 5 4 3 2 1

Library of Congress Cataloging-in-Publication Data

The LCCN for this book is 2003026189
ISBN 0-8248-2839-9

Ke Kaao o Lā'ieikawai by S. N. Hale'ole first appeared in 1863 as a
newspaper serial in the Hawaiian-language newspaper *Ka Nupepa
Kuokoa*. At the conclusion of the series the story was published in
book form by Henry M. Whitney, the newspaper's editor. An English
translation by Margaret W. Beckwith was later published as *The
Hawaiian Romance of Lā'ieikawai* in 1919 by the Bureau of
American Ethnology of the Smithsonian Institution. The text of this
book is an abridged retelling of the legend based upon that English
translation.

University of Hawai'i Press books are printed on acid-free paper and
meet the guidelines for permanence and durability of the Council on
Library Resources

Designed by Santos Barbasa Jr.

To the people of Hawaiʻi,
to their culture,
and to my alma mater,
the University of Hawaiʻi

Contents

FOREWORD

During my seventh-grade year at Kamehameha School in the early 1960s, the author Caroline Curtis would come to our classroom once a month and recount old legends of Hawai'i. The stories she chose were about our ali'i and akua, about men and women in love, about people who could transform into other living beings. She told us vivid and exciting stories about Hawaiians, and she made us feel a connection with those wondrous beings that inhabited these Islands. I do not remember her telling the story of Lā'ieikawai, but it is the kind of story she would tell, and for a few minutes in an otherwise typically dreary day in school, my classmates and I were entranced.

When the venerable Martha Beckwith introduced her early twentieth-century translation of Lā'ieikawai, she described the ways in which this tale had been transformed in its telling Its ancient roots as ka'ao, a spoken fable, distinguished it from the more historical mo'olelo, but its first literary form, written by S. N. Hale'ole in the 1860s, managed to retain the fundamental themes of Hawaiian storytelling: the interrelationships of Nature, gods, and human beings; the prominence of love and physical attraction; the consequences of pettiness and betrayal; and above all, the overwhelming significance of family and relationships.

Dietrich Varez maintains these essential elements in this version. While the narrative is clearly meant to accompany the entrancingly beautiful prints for which he is famous, his story, much like the original *ka'ao*, focuses on those kinds of images that would captivate the mind of a child when told by a master storyteller. Just as the story in its oral form enables the listener to imagine these images through the inflections, emphases, and pauses of the storyteller, Varez's illustrations make it possible for the reader to feel the dramatic beauty of the *'āina* and the people who loved and reveled in it.

Each version of the story of Lā'ieikawai has made the narrative accessible to new audiences. For readers who have never heard the story before, this book will stir them, as these stories have stirred their parents and ancestors, to treasure their Hawaiianness and to value those things about Hawai'i that distinguish this place and our people from everything and everyone else.

Jonathan Kay Kamakawiwo'ole Osorio
Honolulu, Hawai'i

PREFACE

This is an abridged retelling of S. N. Hale'ole's story *The Hawaiian Romance of Lā'ieikawai*, first published in Hawaiian in 1863. A full-length English translation by Martha Beckwith appeared in 1919, and in 1997 a single volume with both Hawaiian and English versions of the legend finally became available.

The wonderful story of Lā'ieikawai is a rare, full-length example of a *ka'ao*, a story passed down orally for generations. With its many colorful characters, intricate plot, and ethnic detail, the story of Lā'ieikawai rivals or even outshines many classic European folktales.

Accompanying this condensed English translation are new illustrations inspired by the wealth of unconventional imagery woven through this timeless tale of old Hawai'i.

Dietrich Varez, 2003

The Legend of
Lāʻieikawai

Two claps of thunder sounded when this story began at Lā'ie, Ko'olau, on the island of O'ahu.

Kahauokapaka was the ruling chief of that district and he very much wanted a son. His wife, Mālaekahana, had given him four daughters but he would not let her keep any of them. The newborn daughters were sent away and the couple remained childless.

Desperate to keep even a girl child for herself Mālaekahana called for the old hunchbacked priest and his wife.

"When next I am about to give birth I will ask my husband to go fishing for the *manini* that I crave. If a girl child is born we will keep her safely hidden with you. When my husband returns from fishing I will tell him the child was stillborn and we have buried it." When her time came and her husband was at sea two claps of thunder sounded. Mālaekahana had given birth to twin girls.

While the echo of the thunder was still trying to find its way out of the mountains the old priest and his wife, Waka, quickly and quietly took away the twin girls.

Mālaekahana had named the girls Lāʻieikawai and Lāʻielohelohe. The old priest took Lāʻielohelohe to the uplands of Wahiawā to the place called Kūkaniloko. There he concealed the child from everyone.

Waka took Lāʻieikawai to a secret cave at the pool called Waiʻāpuka. Because this hiding place could only be reached by diving under the water, Waka was certain that her young charge would be safe there.

But Lāʻieikawai was a special child endowed by the gods with such sacredness that a rainbow constantly arched over her. And soon, the ever-present rainbow gave away her hiding place. Strangers came to the pool at Waiʻāpuka to admire the glorious rainbow. A new hiding place had to be found.

Wily old Waka knew just the place to hide Lāʻieikawai. The idea had come to her in a vision while she slept. The vision told of a wonderful place named Paliuli on the island of Hawaiʻi.

Waka recruited a canoe for the journey and then veiled the young girl's face so that the paddlers might not see her beauty and be roused to gossip as men will do.

After a long and difficult journey, Waka and Lāʻieikawai arrived at Hawaiʻi. The young paddlers had tried every trick they knew to catch a glimpse of the girl's face. The old woman quickly disembarked and escorted Lāʻieikawai out of sight.

From the canoe landing at Keaʻau the pair made their way up through the thick *ʻōhiʻa* forests of Puna to the place called Paliuli. Here, deep in the *ʻōhiʻa* forest, Waka placed Lāʻieikawai in a house made of the yellow feathers of the *ʻōʻō* bird. This was to be their new home.

The lush greenery, abundance of food, and pools of water everywhere made Paliuli a truly wonderful place. It was a paradise. Lāʻieikawai spent her days among the red and yellow *lehua* flowers and colorful birds of the forest. And as always, a brilliant rainbow arched continuously over her yellow feather house.

Unknown to Waka and Lāʻieikawai, new problems were already in the making. Some of the curious canoe paddlers had gotten brief glimpses of Lāʻie's face during the rough channel crossing. Stunned by her beauty, these young men were now spreading the word all around the Islands.

Worst of all, a certain seer named Hulumāniani, who had been intrigued by the ever-present and mysterious rainbow, heard the paddlers' gossip. Seeking to further his own position, the seer sounded his huge drum and told all the chiefs of the land of the beauty of Lāʻieikawai.

Listening to the hypnotic rhythm of the seer's drum and the chant telling of Lāʻieikawai's rank and beauty was the handsome young chief ʻAiwohikupua. He closed his eyes and tried to envision the famed beauty of Paliuli. And suddenly, Lāʻieikawai appeared to him in all her radiance. ʻAiwohikupua was enchanted.

When he awoke from his trance, he tried again to close his eyes and regain the vision of Lāʻieikawai. But it was not to be. Try as he would, he was unable to see the vision again. Lāʻie had escaped him.

Willing to do anything to see Lāʻie's face once more, ʻAiwohikupua tried desperately to dream of her again. He called for his ʻawa chewers and ordered them to prepare the strong narcotic drink so that he might in his drunkenness see the beauty of Lāʻieikawai again. The ʻawa potion worked and ʻAiwohikupua remained in a trance for many days dreaming of Lāʻieikawai. When he awoke, he decided she must be his wife.

'Aiwohi departed immediately to find Lā'ieikawai. He took with him many gifts to persuade the beauty of Paliuli to become his wife. Among the treasures he carried with him was his most prized feather cloak. He intended to impress Lā'ieikawai with his status and high rank as a chief.

En route to Paliuli, 'Aiwohi passed through the district of Kohala, where he saw a crowd of men gathering for a boxing match. The famous boxer Ihuanu was giving an exhibition of his strength. He had already dispatched several challengers.

A clever fellow was this 'Aiwohikupua, and he thought to himself, "If I challenge and defeat this Ihuanu, surely the news will travel around the Islands very quickly. Perhaps even to Paliuli, where Lā'ieikawai will hear of my strength in defeating this champion of Kohala."

Summoning all his skill and strength, 'Aiwohi punched Ihuanu's chest so hard that his fist exited the boxer's back. He was the new champion.

The crowd at the boxing match shouted wildly for the new champion, 'Aiwohikupua. Some men went out right away to find new challengers, but 'Aiwohi refused them. "I must leave now for that rainbow you see there at Paliuli. The woman who lives there is the most beautiful of all and I seek to make her my wife," he said to them.

'Aiwohi's canoe left Kohala and headed for the landing at Kea'au. From Kea'au, 'Aiwohi and his trusted counselor climbed the steep forest trail to the uplands of Paliuli. As they approached Lā'ie's house, 'Aiwohi asked for his precious feather cloak to drape upon his shoulders.

'Aiwohi and the counselor finally reached the clearing in front of Lā'ie's wonderful house thatched with the yellow feathers of the 'ō'ō bird. The chief and his companion were awestruck by the scene. 'Aiwohi's feather cloak seemed a pitiful token in comparison to the magnificent feathered house of the princess. The chief turned and went back into the forest without meeting the princess.

'Aiwohi had been shamed. Lā'ie's yellow feather house caused him to doubt his chances with this rainbow princess of Paliuli. A new plan was needed.

At Kea'au landing, he again boarded his canoe and sailed for Kohala. There he would forget his hurt feelings and enjoy some of his new glory as the local boxing champion.

But 'Aiwohi was still in an amorous mood. He could not forget his love of the woman at Paliuli. This made him particularly vulnerable when he met Poli'ahu, the snow maiden who lived inland at the summit of Mauna Kea.

During his stay at Kohala, 'Aiwohi saw more and more of Poli'ahu. She came to him draped in her white mantle of snow. And he, lovesick as he was, gave her his feather cloak in exchange. They met often among the silversword plants that grew on the cinder slopes of Mauna Kea.

But the embraces of Poliʻahu proved too cold for ʻAiwohi. He still longed for the warmth of Puna and his rainbow princess at Paliuli. Lāʻieikawai was ever on his mind.

Soon he made up a story about trouble between his five sisters on Kauaʻi and told Poliʻahu he would have to leave her briefly to attend to family matters on that island. This was just a clever decoy, however, so that he could plot a new strategy to capture the affections of Lāʻieikawai.

His new plan was to go again to the yellow feather house of Lāʻieikawai but this time with his sisters accompanying him. Their womanly ways, he thought, would help to win over the beautiful rainbow princess and secure her as his wife.

Four of ʻAiwohi's sisters were named after the different kinds of sweet-smelling *maile* plants. The fifth and youngest sister was called Kahalao-māpuana. They all agreed to go with their brother to the place where Lāʻie lived.

After the long voyage from Kaua'i to Kea'au and then the difficult climb up through the *lehua* forest to Paliuli, 'Aiwohi stood once again before the yellow feather house of Lā'ieikawai, this time with his five sisters.

At their brother's urging the four sisters named after the *maile* plants sent forth a wonderful sweet fragrance to charm Lā'ieikawai. The scent filled the forest, Lā'ie's house, and all the surroundings. 'Aiwohi was nearly overcome as he stood and gazed at the entryway to Lā'ie's house.

Inside the house, Lā'ie was awakened by the sweet fragrance coming from the *maile* sisters. The princess called out to her old guardian, Waka. "What is that fragrance, that scent that touches my heart?" she asked the old woman. "It is 'Aiwohikupua and his sisters," said Waka. "He has come to take you as his wife. The *maile* sisters implore you to take him as your husband." "I will not marry him," was Lā'ie's reply. "Tell them to leave us."

Lā'ie's refusal was the final blow to 'Aiwohiku-pua. Standing just outside, he could plainly hear her rejection. Embarrassed before his sisters, the brother dismissed the girls as worthless and stormed away to his canoe.

The sisters ran after their angry brother, but he would not hear them. They pleaded and sang to him in hopes he would be consoled, but he was unmoved.

"Stay here! The forest is your home now! You will live in hollow trees till the end of your days. To me, you are worthless," he said.

At the canoe landing, the sisters again confronted their brother. They sat near the canoe, hoping to be asked aboard. But 'Aiwohikupua would have none of them. "I have no more sisters," he said. In one last attempt the youngest sister, Kahalaomāpuana, clung to the back of 'Aiwohi's departing canoe and pleaded with her brother. He would not even turn to look at her. Kahala released her hold and swam back to shore.

omeless and abandoned by their brother, the five sisters consulted one another about what to do. They decided to return to Paliuli and live near Lāʻieikawai's house. The girls found some hollow trees near the yellow feather house and they lived there in hopes of seeing the princess.

Each night the sisters would light a fire and sit around it singing toward Lāʻieikawai's house. They took turns; a different sister would sing each night. Four nights passed but Lāʻieikawai did not come out of her house. On the fifth night Kahalaomāpuana, the youngest sister, made a little trumpet from a *kī* leaf. She played the instrument with such skill and sweetness that Lāʻieikawai awoke. The princess ordered her guardian to see where the music came from.

"There were five beautiful girls sitting around a fire. The smallest of them played a little *kī* leaf trumpet," the guardian said upon her return to the house.

"Tell them to come into our house," said Lāʻie. "Anyone who can sing and play so sweetly should not have to remain outside. Let us call them in and we will eat and sing together."

Waka, the old guardian, went out to the fire and gave the message to the sisters. The girls were overjoyed and made themselves ready to meet Lāʻieikawai.

They could not believe what they saw when they entered the yellow feather house of Lāʻieikawai. There was the beautiful princess floating on the wings of birds. A *lei* of *lehua* flowers was in her hair and scarlet *ʻiʻiwi* birds fluttered about, tasting the nectar of the blossoms. The girls fell to the ground and humbled themselves before the princess.

"Arise," said Lāʻie. "We will live here together caring for each other as sisters. The birds will bring us food and we will not want anything till the end of our days."

With that Kahalaomāpuana played her sweet trumpet and they all sang and danced late into the night.

In the morning, while the birds were still putting things in order from the previous night's merriment, Lāʻie took the sisters for a walk in the forest. In a cave nearby, she introduced them to Kiha-nuilulumoku, a wondrous, huge, but well-behaved lizard.

"Kiha lives here with us and is our protector. Do not fear her. She will not harm you. Only those who seek to harm us here at Paliuli need fear her. She will surely eat them." And it wasn't long before the sisters had proof of Kiha's awesome power.

'Aiwohikupua, the girls' brother, was still angry over Lāʻie's refusal to become his wife. He plotted revenge and sent forty men with spears to dispatch the girls at Paliuli. "An easy victory," thought the soldiers as they surrounded the yellow feather house with the girls inside. But suddenly Kiha appeared from behind a pile of stones. The soldiers could not believe their eyes. They ran in all directions but Kiha ate them up one by one to the last man.

By the time Lāʻie and the sisters came out of the house to see what the noise was all about, the battle was over. A few splintered spears lay scattered in front of the house. The girls could see Kiha in the distance, sliding back to her cave. "We must stay on guard," Lāʻie said to the sisters. "This brother of yours does not give up easily and he may try to surprise us again."

ʻAiwohikupua meanwhile had heard about the terrible lizard and the defeat of his men. He had one last resort: his marvelous, fearless man-eating dog from Kahiki, Kalahumoku.

ʻAiwohi summoned the dog and carefully instructed him where to find the sisters and Lāʻieikawai. Then, he unleashed Kalahumoku, who ran snarling in the direction of Paliuli. The dog's fate was not much better than that of the forty doomed soldiers. Kalahumoku returned to ʻAiwohikupua several days later. His ears and tail were gone. Kiha had bitten them off.

With his soldiers beaten and his man-eating dog missing its tail and ears, 'Aiwohikupua was thoroughly demoralized. To make matters worse, all this was at the hands of a few girls. It was hard for the chief to accept this defeat and public embarrassment.

'Aiwohikupua resolved to heal his wounds with a more congenial girl. He decided to sail back to Kohala, where he had won the boxing match and met the snow princess Poli'ahu. Poli'ahu would become his wife instead of the elusive Lā'ieikawai.

He ordered the few followers still loyal to him to prepare a large double-hulled canoe for the voyage to Kohala and Poli'ahu. 'Aiwohi wanted to make a good impression on Poli'ahu. He feared the rapidly spreading gossip about his losses to Lā'ieikawai. To dispel any such rumors, he put on the white mantle Poli'ahu had given him and also his helmet made with the red feathers of the 'i'iwi bird.

'Aiwohikupua arrived in grand form. He had brought female dancers with him to perform before Poli'ahu. And he had clothed his followers and canoe paddlers in red and white *kapa* to match his own cape and feather helmet.

Poli'ahu was impressed and overjoyed that this handsome chief had returned for her. She even agreed to become his wife and return to Kaua'i with him.

On the night before their wedding, 'Aiwohikupua and Poli'ahu were entertaining some friends with the *kilu* game and the *kā'eke* dance. The *kilu* game, resembling "spin-the-bottle," was accompanied by much whispering and gossip. It was then that Poli'ahu was made aware of 'Aiwohikupua's womanizing ways.

She became very angry with the chief and caused him to feel her coldness. Poli'ahu withdrew from 'Aiwohi and rejected him. She left him forever and returned to her snow-covered mountain top to live alone among the silverswords.

That was nearly the last anyone heard about 'Aiwohikupua. The devastated chief decided to remain secluded and out of public life.

It was during this time that Lā'ieikawai and the sisters had taken to surfing at Kea'au. A particularly handsome youth named Halaaniani also surfed there and soon was admiring the beautiful girl from Paliuli. Halaaniani had a reputation for flirting with the girls at the beach, but he was ashamed to approach Lā'ieikawai and did not speak to her.

Instead Halaaniani asked his sister, Mali'o, a sorceress of sorts, to aid him in winning Lā'ieikawai for himself. Mali'o, who could perform all sorts of wondrous deeds, agreed to help her brother.

"Tomorrow when you are surfing near the rainbow princess I will cause a mist to come over both of you," said Mali'o. "The princess will not be able to resist you and you can have your way with her. No one will see you."

And it was just as Mali'o had said. The mist came over Lā'ieikawai and Halaaniani as they rode the great wave together. No one saw them. When the mist cleared, only their surfboards remained on the beach.

Halaaniani and Lā'ieikawai had gone to Paliuli together. They were exhausted from surfing and rested in Lā'ieikawai's yellow feather house. Here they entertained each other and became very close friends.

But in the morning a terrible thing happened. Old Waka, the guardian grandmother, came into the house and saw Halaaniani with Lā'ieikawai. The old woman flew into a rage and wailed and shouted.

Old Waka had hoped to have Lā'ieikawai married to a chief of high rank. This would have brought blessings for the old grandmother also. But now, in one careless moment, Lā'ieikawai had been spoiled by a mere surfer.

Waka was furious. She chided Lā'ieikawai and disowned the rainbow princess. The old woman's motives were clearly showing. She had hoped to have someone care for her in her old age but now all that was changed. She cursed the surfer Halaaniani.

Soon Waka had devised a new plan. She prepared for a journey to O'ahu to the place where Lā'ieikawai's twin sister, Lā'ielohelohe, had been hidden since birth.

Waka brought a little pig with her and offered it to Lā'ielohelohe's guardian while she related the story of Lā'ieikawai's fall. The old guardian was pleased with the pig and sympathetic to Waka's tale. He agreed to let Lā'ielohelohe go with Waka to replace Lā'ieikawai at Paliuli.

Waka quickly had a new house built just like the one Lā'ieikawai lived in. She moved Lā'ielohelohe into it and told Lā'ieikawai to stay away from her innocent twin sister.

The surfer Halaaniani meanwhile was still coming up to Paliuli, where he had met with Lā'ieikawai. But now he was enamored with a new girl. He had spotted Lā'ieikawai's twin sister. Lā'ielohelohe often wandered through the *lehua* forest of Paliuli gathering blossoms for her adornment. Waka had found a husband for the girl and prepared for a wedding. Betrothed to a high chief, Lā'ielohelohe was avoiding contact with all others until after her marriage.

But Halaaniani would not stay away. Again he asked his sister Mali'o to help him steal this girl, too.

Mali'o devised a clever plot to snare the twin of Lā'ieikawai for her brother. "When next you see Lā'ielohelohe gathering the *lehua* blossoms, hide yourself up in one of the nearby trees," she told her brother. "When the girl passes right under where you are hidden, drop a bunch of flowers in front of her. Meanwhile I will be nearby playing a soothing tune on my magic noseflute."

Halaaniani climbed a tree, hid himself, and tried the trick Mali'o had suggested. As Lā'ielohelohe approached, Mali'o played a soft, enchanting tune on her magic flute.

Lā'ielohelohe was startled at the sound of the music and looked up as Halaaniani's flowers fell in front of her. But she was not deceived. Old Waka had told her all about the good-looking young surfer who had stolen Lā'ieikawai.

"You should not be here," she said to Halaaniani and Mali'o. "I am to be wed to the high chief Kekalukaluokewā tomorrow and if he knows of your presence here, you will surely be punished."

Mali'o and her eager brother did not need to be reminded twice of what would befall them should they be caught. The surfer jumped out of his tree and left quickly. Mali'o followed without delay.

Meanwhile, a great feast was being laid out for the marriage of Lā'ielohelohe to the chief Kekalukaluokewā.

no one had ever seen a wedding like it. The best of everything was there: roasted pig, breadfruit, bananas, fish, both raw and cooked, sweet potatoes, *poi*, and *ʻopihi.*

Lāʻielohelohe and her chiefly husband sat at the head of the feast. Everyone had been invited. There were dancers to perform for the guests and great merriment for all.

Even Lāʻieikawai and the five sisters had been invited. Lāʻielohelohe loved her twin sister and had pleaded with her new husband to let Lāʻieikawai attend.

But no one could have anticipated how Lāʻieikawai would arrive. The forest around the wedding feast parted and the great lizard Kiha appeared. And there, riding on the outstretched tongue of the immense lizard, sat Lāʻieikawai surrounded by her birds.

The wedding guests were awed. Some were even fearful. But when they saw the lizard meant them no harm, the festivities resumed and carried on late into the night.

In the days that followed the wedding of her sister, Lāʻieikawai's moods were uncertain. She was happy for her twin sister's good fortune. But she was also sad for her own lot. Life at Paliuli was not the same.

Kahalaomāpuana noticed Lāʻie's melancholy and spoke with the other girls. "Our sister longs for a husband of her own. Let us see what we can do for her."

"Your sadness touches us all," they said to Lāʻieikawai. "We have agreed to find a new husband for you so that our household will again be at peace."

It was then that Kahalaomāpuana told of another brother, Kaʻōnohiokalā, the Eyeball of the Sun, who would be a suitable husband for Lāʻieikawai. The young sister offered to make the long journey to the Sun to bring back Kaʻōnohiokalā for Lāʻieikawai. The great lizard was called out once more and the small young sister climbed up on Kiha's gigantic back to begin her journey to the Sun.

As everyone knows, however, a journey to the Sun is no easy matter, even for a great lizard. Kiha and Kahala had to first cross the ocean to reach Keʻalohilani, the Shining Heavens. It took them four months and ten days just to do that.

From there they went on to Nuʻumealani, the Raised Place in the Heavens. After ten more days of travel, Kahalaomāpuana and the great lizard reached the place where they could ascend the heavens.

Suddenly there was a shadow across the sky and the great cosmic ancestral spider, Lanalananuiʻaumakua, appeared. Kahala called out to the spider to let down its web so that she might climb up. Slowly the web spun down until Kahala could grasp it while standing upon Kiha's back. Without fear Kahala stepped onto the spider's web and began the long climb up toward the Sun. Far below, she could still see the great lizard looking up.

Kahalaomāpuana climbed the spider's web for a whole day. At night, she finally came into the shadow of the moon. This was the land of Kahakaekaea.

The first thing she saw was a house standing by a garden patch. At first no one seemed to be there, but then she spotted an old man with a very long gray beard. He was sleeping on a mound of sweet potato plants.

"This is no ordinary old man," Kahala thought to herself. "Surely he will know the way to Ka'ōnohiokalā, my brother who lives in the Sun."

Quietly, the girl approached the sleeping old man. His face was turned up and his long gray beard lay across his chest.

Kahala gripped the old man's beard and sat upon him so that he could not get up. She pulled and twisted his beard, all the while asking him directions to find her brother.

The old man was shocked to find this brazen girl sitting on him, tugging his beard and asking all those questions. After shouting and arguing for a while, the groggy old man finally told the girl what she wanted.

"I can't help you find your brother but my wife can," he yelled out. "She is down by the river where the bamboo grows. She is making some *kapa* there."

"How will your wife know where to find Ka'ōnohiokalā?" the girl persisted. "She is his mother," the old man replied. It was then that Kahalaomāpuana realized that the old man was her father and his wife, her mother. She apologized for her rudeness and they embraced each other.

Then Kahalaomāpuana hurried down to the river, where she found Laukiele'ula, her mother, pounding out her *kapa* by some rocks. They, too, embraced and Kahala told her mother of her purpose.

Laukiele'ula listened carefully to her daughter's plan to retrieve a husband for Lā'ieikawai. And the mother agreed that Ka'ōnohiokalā would be a suitable choice.

"Let us go up to where he lives," the mother said. She began a chant that Kahala had never heard before. The chant called for the Halulu bird that would carry them up to Awakea, where Ka'ōnohiokalā lived.

The two women sat upon the great bird's wings as it gracefully flew ever higher up into the noonday.

As they neared the Sun, Kahala could feel the increasing heat. It was almost unbearable. Just when she thought she would have to stop, Laukiele'ula reached out and seized one of the Sun's rays. The heat immediately stopped and a cool shade surrounded them.

There, sitting sleepily in the very center of the Sun, was Ka'ōnohiokalā. He greeted his mother and embraced his sister and asked why they had come.

The huge Halulu bird made a few more circles around the Sun and then disappeared. Kahalaomāpuana explained her mission to her brother.

"And that is why I've come, to ask you to become husband to my mistress at Paliuli. There is none more beautiful than Lāʻieikawai, the rainbow princess. Should you consent, I will return to tell her of your decision."

And Kahalaomāpuana also told of the wickedness of ʻAiwohikupua, Waka, Halaaniani, and Maliʻo.

"They will all be punished when I come down to take Lāʻieikawai to be my wife," said Kaʻōnohiokalā. "Go back now and prepare for my arrival and the marriage of Lāʻieikawai."

Then Kaʻōnohiokalā held forth his hand and gave his young sister a rainbow to give to Lāʻieikawai so that he would know his wife by this sign. Kahala was overjoyed with the success of the mission and made her return to Lāʻieikawai.

Kahalaomāpuana had been back with Lāʻieika-wai only a short while when Kaʻōnohiokalā arrived to take his bride.

Kaʻōnohiokalā had assumed his mortal state as a chief of high rank for this visit. He left his blinding heat back at home in the center of the Sun.

His very first actions were to punish Waka and ʻAiwohikupua for their wrongs. All the others received their punishment in turn. Finally, he placed Kahalaomāpuana as ruler over separate islands.

Lāʻieikawai and Kaʻōnohiokalā then went up upon a rainbow to the land within the clouds, where they lived as husband and wife.

At times Kaʻōnohi would have to leave their heavenly home to oversee affairs down below. Such visits were required of a ruling chief of his stature. It was on one of these visits below that he fell in love with his wife's sister, Lāʻielohelohe.

oon Ka'ōnohi's visits below became more and more frequent. Each visit took longer than the previous one. But Lā'ieikawai suspected nothing of her husband's affairs down below.

Ka'ōnohiokalā had meanwhile cleverly arranged for Lā'ielohelohe's husband to be away. He sent the husband, Kekalukaluokewā, on a tour of inspection of all the Islands. This would take a long time, thereby giving Ka'ōnohiokalā plenty of opportunity to further his lot with Lā'ielohelohe.

It was after Ka'ōnohi had been away from Lā'ieikawai for over a year that the rainbow princess began to get suspicious. She asked her parents, "How may I see what is going on below?" The old parents brought forth a huge gourd named Laukapalili. "You must look into the gourd and quietly whisper its name. Then all will be revealed to you," they told her. Lā'ieikawai then saw her husband caressing Lā'ielohelohe down below.

And the old parents also saw what the gourd Laukapalili had revealed. They were grieved to see their son flirting and carrying on with Lāʻielohelohe.

Lāʻieikawai was saddened by what the gourd had revealed, especially because her sister was involved. Lāʻie decided to consult with the old parents about what they should do. It was decided Kaʻōnohiokalā would be banned from living in the heavens because he had defiled himself and his household.

The old parents used their supernatural powers to deny Kaʻōnohiokalā access to the pathway to the heavens. He could no longer return to his heavenly home.

"Your name will be Lapu, a ghost," they told him. "You will be a ghost, wandering the roads from place to place. And you will be fearsome to all. Worst of all you are condemned to eat moths as your food for the rest of your life." So they said to Kaʻōnohiokalā and then left him alone forever.

With Kaʻōnohiokalā banished, the old parents called for Kahalaomāpuana. They took her to fill Kaʻōnohi's place in the heavens. For some time, Lāʻieikawai and Kahalaomāpuana consoled each other in their sorrow. Life was pleasant and trouble free in this high place.

But Lāʻieikawai was lonely. She enjoyed having Kahala there, but longed to be with her twin sister.

"Your sister has been defiled by Kaʻōnohiokalā and therefore cannot live here in the heavens," the parents told her. "But there is nothing to keep you from going below to live there with her. That is your decision to make."

And so Lāʻieikawai decided to leave her place in the heavens and return to Earth below to live with her twin sister Lāʻielohelohe. She was then no longer known as Lāʻieikawai. Her name became Kawahineokaliʻulā.

And from that time to this she is still worshiped as "the Woman of the Twilight."

Glossary of Characters, Place Names, and Hawaiian Terms

CHARACTERS

'Aiwohikupua: Chief of Kaua'i, suitor to Lā'ieikawai.

Halaaniani: A young surfer.

Halulu: A giant legendary mythical bird.

Hulumāniani: A seer from Kaua'i.

Ihuanu: A boxing champion from Kohala.

Kahalaomāpuana: Youngest sister of 'Aiwohikupua.

Kahauokapaka: Father of Lā'ieikawai.

Kalahumoku: Fighting dog of 'Aiwohikupua.

Ka'ōnohiokalā: "The eyeball of the sun." A chief from Kahiki.

Kawahineokali'ulā: The name Lā'ieikawai took after returning to live with her sister.

Kekalukaluokewā: A chief and suitor to Lā'ielohelohe.

Kihanuilulumoku: A giant supernatural guardian lizard.

Lā'ieikawai: Heroine of the story, "'Ie Leaf in the Water."

Lā'ielohelohe: Twin sister of Lā'ieikawai.

Lanalananui'aumakua: A giant mythical cosmic spider.

Laukiele'ula: Mother of Kahalaomāpuana.

Mālaekahana: Mother of Lā'ieikawai.

Mali'o: A sorceress.

Poli'ahu: A snow princess.

Waka: A sorceress, Grandmother of Lā'ieikawai.

PLACE NAMES

Hawai'i: Largest island of the Hawaiian group.

Kahakaekaea: A mythical place in the heavens.

Kahiki: An ancestral mythical place.

Kaua'i: Island of the Hawaiian group.

Kea'au: Land section on the island of Hawai'i.

Ke'alohilani: A mythical place in the heavens.

Kohala: Land district on the island of Hawai'i.

Ko'olau: A windward district on the island of O'ahu.

Kūkaniloko: A district on O'ahu where royalty gave birth.

Lā'ie: A land district on the island of O'ahu.

Mauna Kea: A mountain on the island of Hawai'i.

Nu'umealani: A mythical place in the heavens.

O'ahu: Most populous island of the Hawaiian group.

Paliuli: A legendary paradise of abundance in Puna.

Puna: Land district on the island of Hawai'i.

Wahiawā: Land district on the island of O'ahu.

Wai'āpuka: A pond at Lā'ie on the island of O'ahu.

HAWAIIAN TERMS

'Awa: A plant used to make a narcotic drink.

'I'iwi: A red-feathered Hawaiian forest bird.

Kā'eke: Bamboo pipes used in making music.

Kapa or tapa: Hawaiian barkcloth.

Kī: The ti plant, used for ceremonial, culinary, and utilitarian purposes.

Kilu: A kissing game similar to "spin-the-bottle."

Lapu: Ghost.

Laukapalili: A gourd calabash used to reveal events.

Lehua: Blossoms of the 'ōhi'a tree.

Lei: A floral garland.

Maile: A vine with fragrant leaves.

Manini: A type of surgeonfish.

'Ōhi'a: A common tree in Hawaiian forests.

'Ō'ō: An extinct Hawaiian forest bird.

'Opihi: Limpet, a seafood delicacy.

Poi: The Hawaiian staple food made from the taro plant.

About the Author/Illustrator

Dietrich Varez has lived in the Hawaiian Islands since he was eight years old. He spent his first years on the island of Oʻahu, where he attended Roosevelt High School and later graduated from the University of Hawaiʻi at Mānoa. After two years in the Army, he returned to the University of Hawaiʻi and worked as a graduate assistant in the English department. In 1968 Dietrich and his wife, Linda (also an artist), moved to the island of Hawaiʻi and purchased nine acres of secluded rain forest on the slopes of Kīlauea Volcano. The land, which lies at nearly 4,000 feet, is several rugged miles from the village of Volcano and the entrance to Hawaiʻi Volcanoes National Park. A self-taught artist, Dietrich began selling his distinctive linoleum-block prints at the Volcano Art Center Gallery in 1974.

Inspired by the natural beauty of the ʻōhiʻa forests surrounding his home and by the power of Hawaiian culture and legends, Dietrich Varez has provided illustrations for a number of important books, most notably *ʻŌlelo Noʻeau: Hawaiian Proverbs and Poetical Sayings* translated by Mary Kawena Pukui, *Māui the Demigod* by Steven

Goldsberry, and *A Legendary Tradition of Kamapua'a, the Hawaiian Pig-God* by Lilikala K. Kame'eleihiwa. In addition, he has retold and illustrated the legends of *Pele the Fire Goddess*, *Māui the Mischief Maker*, and *Hina the Goddess*.

Production Notes for *The Legend of Lāʻieikawai*
    by Dietrich Varez

Cover and interior design, and composition
    by Santos Barbasa Jr.

Illustrations by Dietrich Varez